DEEP OCEAN CREATURES

By Lisa L. Ryan-Herndon

SCHOLASTIC INC.
New York Toronto London Auckland
Sydney Mexico City New Delhi Hong Kong

Photo Copyright Credits

Front Cover: Norbert Wu/Minden Pictures

Back Cover: Charles Hood/Oceans Image/PhotoShot

Title page: Norbert Wu/Minden Pictures; Pages 2-3: Frank & Joyce Burek/Photodisc (provided by BBC Planet Earth); Pages 4-5: F. Ehrenstrom/OSF/Animals Animals; Pages 6-7: Norbert Wu/Minden Pictures; Page 8: Konstantin Inozemtsev/iStockPhoto; Page 9: Peter Arnold/Alamy; Pages 10-11:Denis Scott/Corbis; Page 12: Reinhard Diescher/ Visuals Unlimited; Page 13: Frank & Joyce Burek/Photodisc (provided by BBC Planet Earth); Page 14: Reuters; Page 15: Norbert Wu/Minden Pictures/National Geographic; Pages 16-17: Bruce Rasner/Rotman/Nature Picture Library; Page 18: Masa Uchioda/SeaPics.com; Page 19: Brian J. Skerry/National Geographic; Pages 20-21: Doug Perrine/SeaPics.com; Page 22: Sinclair Stammers/Minden; Page 23: Kevin Raskoff 2005; Page 24: David Shale/ Nature Picture Library; Page 25: Brad Seibel; Page 26: Solvin Zankl/Nature Picture Library; Page 27: Norbert Wu/ Minden Pictures; Page 28: Nikita Tiunov/Shutterstock; Page 29: Charles Hood/Oceans Image/PhotoShot

Photo research: Lois Safrani, Els Rijper

ISBN-13: 978-0-545-11208-6
ISBN-10: 0-545-11208-7

12 11 10 9 8 7 6 5 4 40 11 12 13 14/0

Printed in the U.S.A.

First printing, September 2009

Printed on paper containing minimum of 30% post-consumer fiber.

Contents

Under the Sea

The ocean covers more than half of our planet. Sea life can exist even at the ocean's greatest depths, where not even humans can travel. There are millions of miles of ocean floor and creatures that have yet to be discovered.

The deep ocean is the world's largest **habitat**, but the most difficult for humans to explore. On the sea floor, the water pressure is 300 times greater than it is at the surface.

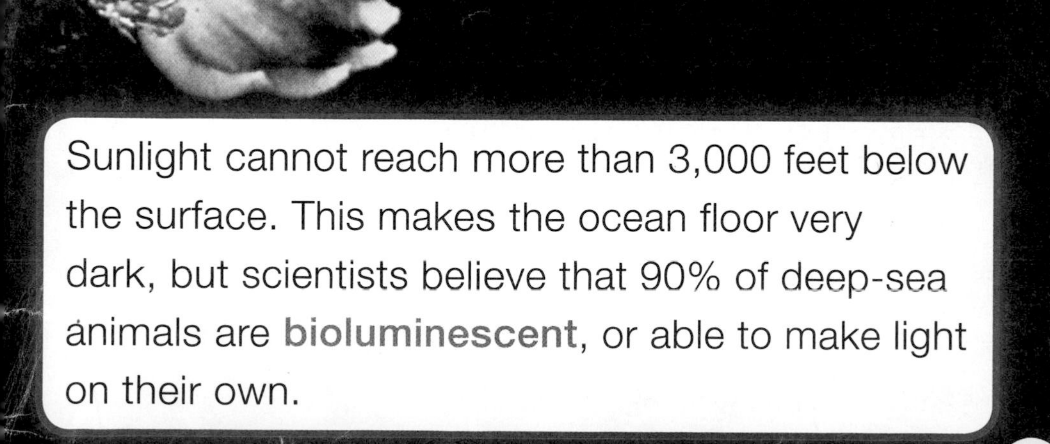

Sunlight cannot reach more than 3,000 feet below the surface. This makes the ocean floor very dark, but scientists believe that 90% of deep-sea animals are **bioluminescent**, or able to make light on their own.

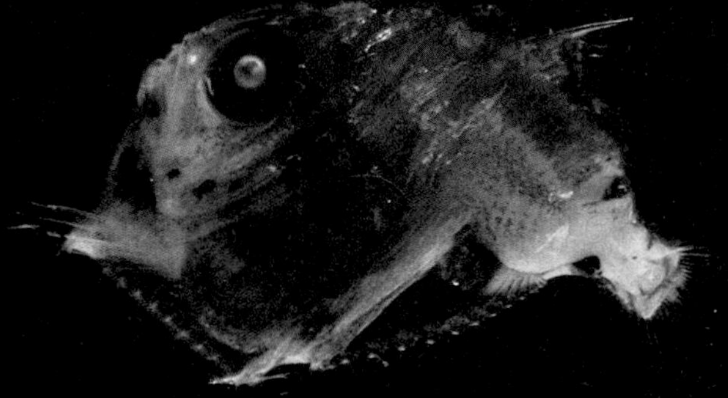

Ocean animals can be placed into three groups: floaters, swimmers, and deep-sea crawlers that live on the sea floor. Floaters, like **plankton**, are pushed along by the tide while swimmers include animals like fish, whales, and seals. Deep-sea creatures, like the spider crab, cling to rocks or reefs, or move along the ocean floor.

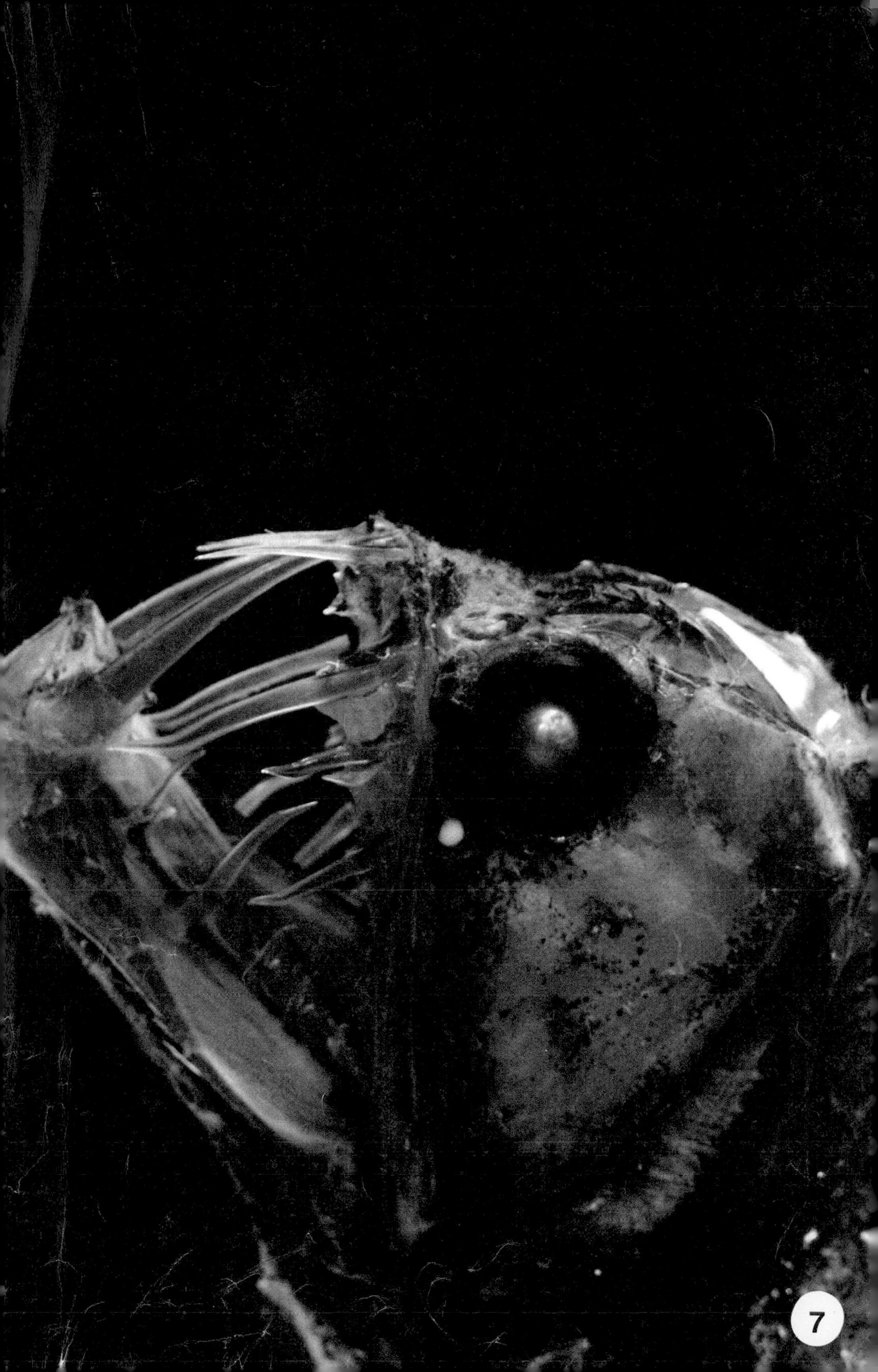

PHYTOPLANKTON

Marine life have their own **food chain**, starting with tiny life-forms called plankton, or phytoplankton. **Algae** are an example of a type of plankton that need sunlight; therefore, they can often be found floating near the ocean's surface.

ZOOPLANKTON

Zooplankton or animals such as worms and jellyfish can move all throughout the ocean. They eat plants but can also be eaten by other marine life themselves.

BLUE WHALE

The blue whale is the largest animal in the world and can weigh up to 200 tons! That's twice the size of the biggest dinosaur. Its heart is the size of a small sports car and its tail is the same width as the wings of a small airplane.

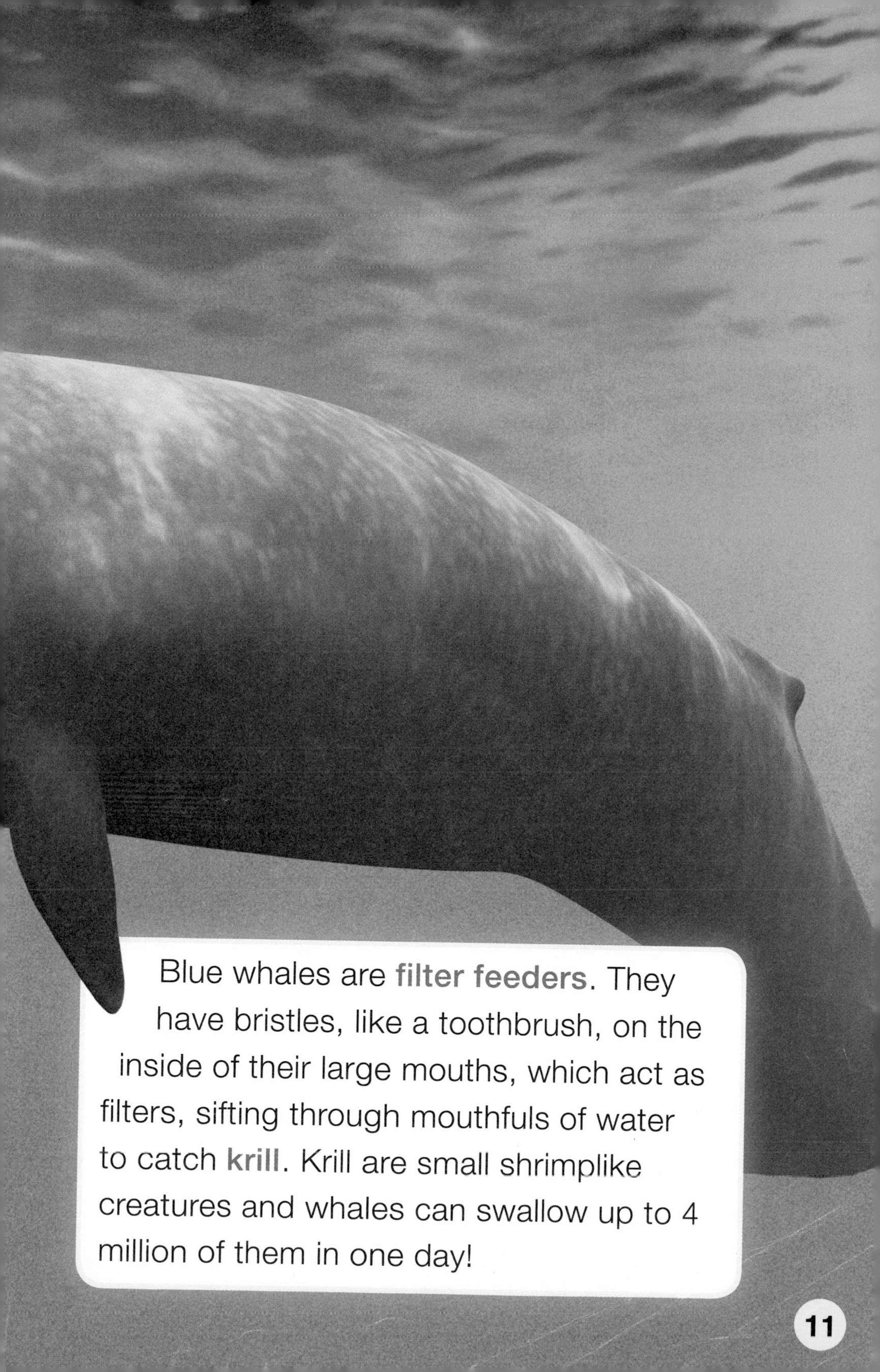

Blue whales are **filter feeders**. They have bristles, like a toothbrush, on the inside of their large mouths, which act as filters, sifting through mouthfuls of water to catch **krill**. Krill are small shrimplike creatures and whales can swallow up to 4 million of them in one day!

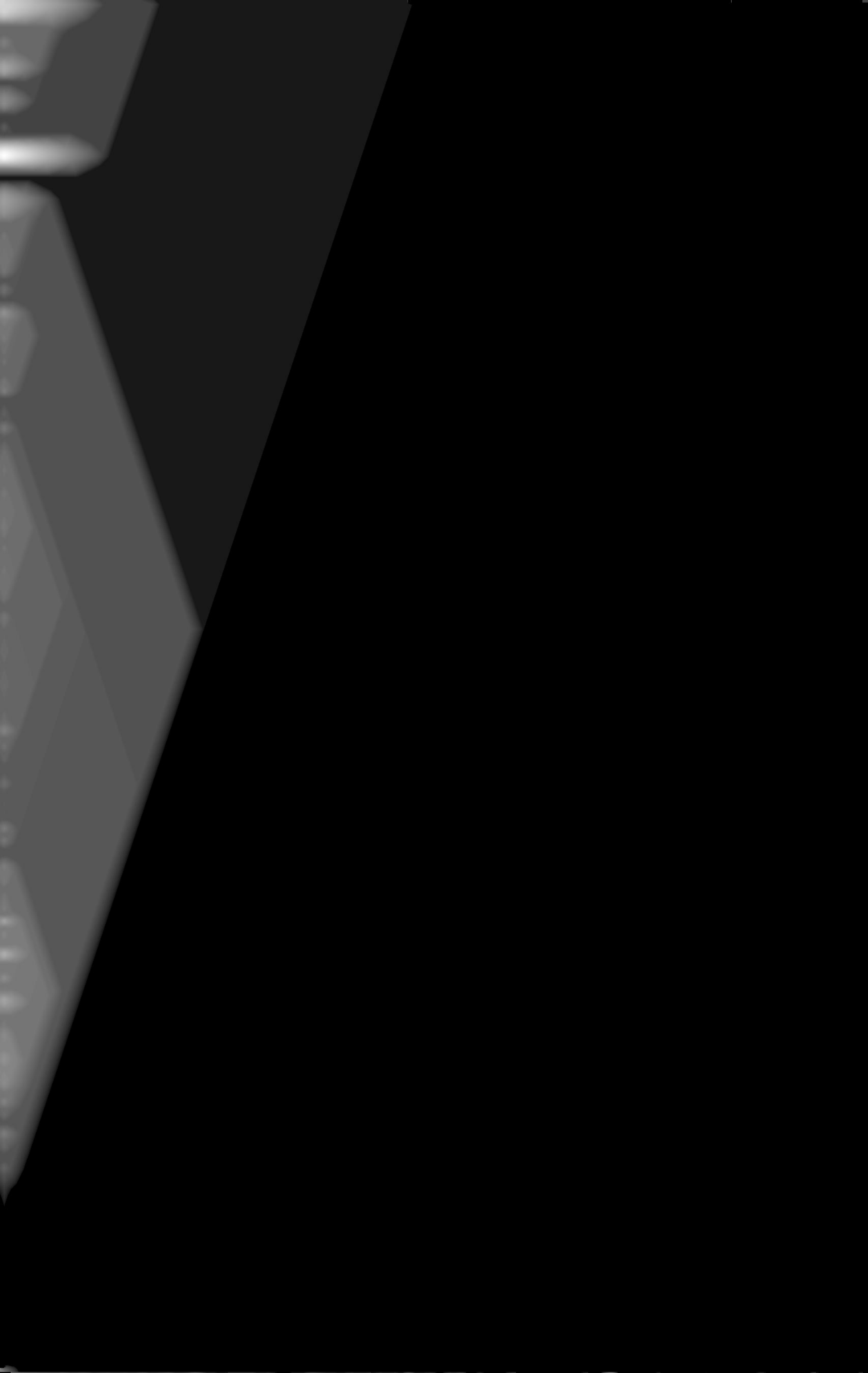

GREEN SEA TURTLE

The sea turtle's green color comes from eating algae.

The green turtle was made for life at sea. Their greenish-brown upper shell is wide and smooth and they have flippers shaped like paddles, which make them powerful swimmers. They can reach speeds of up to 35 miles per hour.

NAUTILUS

The shell of the nautilus has gas-filled organs to help it move up or down.

During the day, the nautilus can be found 1,800 feet below the ocean surface, but at night this swimmer will make its way to the reefs to look for food. The nautilus has 90 **tentacles** that can sense food or danger, such as a hungry octopus.

Hide or Hunt

Millions of sea creatures are trying to survive in the deep ocean. **Predators** often have a better chance of finding food closer to the surface where there are few places to hide.

MEGAMOUTH SHARK

The megamouth shark is rarely spotted as it lives at depths of 490 to 3,300 feet in the ocean. You can see from its giant mouth where this shark got its name. The megamouth is one of three filter feeder sharks in the sea, along with the whale shark and the basking shark.

MANTA RAY

Manta rays swoop and glide on 26-foot-wide wings and can weigh more than two tons! These warm-water rays are also filter feeders. They use blade-shaped fins on their heads to steer plankton into their mouths.

OCEANIC WHITETIP SHARK

The whitetip shark is considered the most dangerous shark of all!

The oceanic whitetip shark is easily recognized by the white tips on its rounded fins. This shark uses its sense of smell to hunt near the **equator**'s warm waters. The whitetips will often follow schools of fish such as tuna to feed from.

The sailfish has a bony spear for a nose and is named after its **dorsal fin** — the larger, sail-like fin on its back. At about 5 feet long and approximately 132 pounds, this swimmer can zoom by at a speed of up to 68 miles per hour, making it the world's fastest fish. The sailfish is never late for dinner!

Teams of sailfish find and herd fish into a circle, or "bait ball." Waving their fins like flags, the sailfish team drives the bait ball upwards — where the frigate birds wait to share the meal.

COMB JELLY

Comb jellies eat other comb jellies!

A comb jelly is a cousin to the jellyfish. Its clear, round body is 95 percent water. Its name comes from eight rows of **cilia**, hundreds of tiny hairs that act like paddles to push it along. About 90 different kinds of comb jellies roam the oceans.

SIPHONOPHORE

Siphonophores can grow more than 100 feet long.

A siphonophore looks like a jellyfish. Each part of the siphonophore has a job: glow, catch, eat or sting. The most famous siphonophore is the Portuguese man-of-war, which floats near the surface. Other siphonophores hunt anywhere from 2,000 feet below the surface down to the ocean floor.

DUMBO OCTOPUS

The dumbo octopus is named after its huge, earlike fins. It slowly flaps these ears to move through the deepest parts of the oceans, where all 37 species of its group lives. Its large eyes are great for hunting worms and shellfish on the ocean floor.

VAMPIRE SQUID

The vampire squid makes its home more than 9,000 feet below the ocean's surface. If threatened, the squid will eject a sticky cloud of mucus that emits blue light to try and shock predators, allowing it to disappear into the blackness of the ocean depths and out of danger!

Down in the deepest ocean depths, miles away from sunlight, fish have very striking features like big eyes, large mouths, and long sharp teeth. These characteristics along with keen senses help sea life such as the viperfish find food in this scarce environment.

ANGLERFISH

The anglerfish, or monkfish, is the best fisherman in the sea. It doesn't chase food. It digs into the sandy ocean floor and waves its own built-in, shiny, fishing pole or **lure**. The lure glows because of bioluminescent bacteria on its tip. Other fish want a closer look at the shiny object and . . . GULP! The anglerfish has caught its dinner.

SEA CUCUMBER

Leftover dinners eaten near the ocean's surface eventually fall like snow to the ocean floor. Sea cucumbers, urchins, spiders, crabs, conger eels, and shrimp wait months for a meal to finally hit bottom. Every crumb will be eaten. These animals are **scavengers**, and they act as the ocean's clean-up crew.

SPIDER CRAB

Scavengers like the spider crab are always in search of their next meal. At three feet wide, this **crustacean** uses its long legs to move quickly along the ocean floor. The spider crab can detect the faintest of tastes in the water and quickly locate a sinking meal.

Algae – small plants without stems or roots that develop on wet surfaces or in water.

Bioluminescent – the ability that some deep-sea creatures have to make their own light.

Cilia – tiny hairs.

Crustacean – animals that have an outer skeleton and live in the sea.

Dorsal fin – the main fin on the back of an animal that helps with balance.

Equator – an imaginary line halfway between the North and South poles around the center of the world.

Filter feeders – animals that eat by passing water that contains small animal and plant life through its mouth.

Food chain – an arrangement of plants and animals where each feeds on the one beneath it in the chain.

Habitat – the place and environment where a plant or an animal lives.

Krill – tiny shrimplike animals that float in oceans.

Lure – to attract and lead a creature into a trap.

Plankton – tiny plants and animals that drift in lakes and oceans.

Predators – animals that hunt other animals for food.

Scavengers – animals that will eat the remains of other animals' meals.

Tentacles – flexible, long limbs of some animals used for feeling, moving, and grasping.

There is only one Planet Earth

Down the Tubes. Why not shut off the faucet when you're brushing your teeth? You'll save lots of water from going down the drain.

Just Say No to Plastic Water Bottles. Instead of using disposable plastic water bottles, get a reusable container to bring water with you.

Remember the Three R's. Reduce. Reuse. Recycle.